Eid Empanadas

Enjoy all of Wendy Díaz's books

Wendy Díaz

Eid Empanadas

Illustrated by
Uthman Guadalupe

ISBN: 9798748362757

Dedication

To my family,

Who, despite their love for my empanadas, support

me when I choose writing over cooking.

Introduction

Dear Reader,

Are you ready to learn all about the Islamic festival of Eid and what it could possibly have to do with *empanadas,* a traditional Latin-American food staple?

The story you are about to embark on contains some Spanish words and Islamic terminology. You can use context clues to help you figure out the meaning of these words. I have also added a glossary of Spanish words and Islamic terms that you can use as a reference at the back of the book. Try your best to guess the definition of the words before checking the glossary. You will be surprised how much you will already know just from reading the story!

I have also included a bonus and a surprise at the end of the book. Hey, no peeking! Read the story first before you see the surprise! A prize without some effort is not exciting at all.

Thank you for taking the time to read this book! I hope you enjoy it.

With love,

Wendy Díaz

Contents

1. THE ASSIGNMENT

"RAMADAN IS ALMOST HERE!" Ms. Khan exclaimed joyfully. "It is time to celebrate the revelation of our Holy Book, the Qur'an, and then after that comes our big Eid holiday. Who is excited?"

Her students eagerly stretched and wiggled their hands in the air, and in unison, shouted, "ME, ME, MEEEEEE!" It was a Thursday morning, and the month of Ramadan was set to begin Sunday or Monday, depending on when the new moon was sighted.

Ms. Khan, the 4th grade English teacher at An-Noor Islamic Academy, smiled. She paced back and forth in front of her colorfully decorated classroom, and she cheerfully responded, "Me too! And you know what? This is my favorite time of the year. I look forward to it every time."

She clasped her hands together and opened her black kohl-lined eyes wide as she leaned forward to ask, "What do you like most about Ramadan?"

"The food!" Ayesha shouted from the back right corner of the room. "Yeah!" Everyone agreed as she covered her mouth, realizing she forgot to raise her hand and be called on before blurting out her answer. Ms. Khan laughed.

"The food? But Ramadan is about fasting, so how can the best thing be the food?" She asked while scratching her chin and wrinkling her nose. The children giggled. "Fasting means that you cannot eat or drink. During Ramadan, Muslims do not eat or drink from dawn until sunset. Once the sun goes down, we can finally eat, and, usually, families have a meal together before heading out to pray."

Ms. Khan wrote on the board in capital letters, RAMADAN, as she spoke, "My favorite part of Ramadan is the *Tarawih* prayers at night. I love going over the whole Quran in prayer, all 30 parts during the Ramadan nights.

How about you Abdullah, what is your favorite part of Ramadan?" She asked as she approached his desk.

A young boy with caramel skin and eyes to match responded shyly, "I like to go to the *masjid* with my dad. I get to see all my friends."

"Ah, yes, that is fun," Agreed Ms. Khan. "And how does your family prepare for Ramadan? Anyone want to share?" She looked around the room as some of her students, like Ali, Maryam, Mustafa, and Haifa, raised their hands. "Hmm," she put her hand on her chin again. Omar crouched down into his seat, avoiding eye contact, hoping that Ms. Khan would not call his name.

She glanced over to him but quickly noticed that he did not want to be called. She said, "Ok, class, how about you write about how your family celebrates Ramadan as your homework assignment for tonight? Then you can each present your paper in front of the class."

"Awww!" protested some of the students. Omar pressed his cheek on the palm of one hand and rubbed the front of his forehead with the other. "Oh boy," he sighed to himself.

Ms. Khan continued, "Insha'Allah, God willing, tomorrow, we can share all about how our families celebrate Ramadan. Maybe you can give me some new ideas on how I can get ready for this blessed month!" She wrote the assignment on the board for the children to copy into their agendas.

"HOW DOES YOUR FAMILY CELEBRATE RAMADAN? Write at least five paragraphs. Due tomorrow!"

2. EXTRA HELP

WHEN IT WAS TIME FOR RECESS, the children went out to the schoolyard. Omar kicked the rocks from the pavement of the basketball court onto the sandy dirt of the playground.

It was his second year in the private Islamic school, and he was still getting used to the environment. Prior to that, he was in a public school where most of the kids shared the same background, although most were not Muslim.

Omar thought about Ms. Khan's assignment. What could he write? "The way my family prepares for Ramadan is going to be so much different than everyone else," he thought, "No one will understand."

He walked over to his friends, Jamil and Sami, who were desperately trying to shoot basketballs into the nearest hoop on the blacktop.

Omar continued looking down until his friends noticed he was not insisting on having a turn.

"What's up, Omar?" asked Jamil, raising his eyebrow. "Something wrong?"

Omar tried to shake off his worries, "Nah… um… Can I ask you something?"

"Sure. What is it?" Jamil responded. He held a basketball between his right arm and rib cage while Sami tossed another ball over the hoop.

"What does your family do for Ramadan?" asked Omar, rushing through the words trying to sound casual. Maybe his friends could give him some ideas.

"Oh, well, we just do the same thing every year… You know?" Jamil shrugged, "My mom cooks a lot. She goes to the African grocery store and buys all the ingredients she needs to make dishes from our country. My family back home sends us clothes. Everyone takes out their Quran to read and their beads they use to count blessings after their prayers. My dad makes me read Qur'an to my…"

Sami interrupted, "Yea, my family does the same thing, except they make Egyptian food. Stuffed grape leaves, ta'ameya, koushery, mulukhiya, fattah…"

Omar and Jamil wrinkled their noses, trying to understand all the different names. "Fat… what?" Jamil laughed, "Fat-ah is what you're gonna be after you eat all that food!"

Sami grinned. "I haven't even gotten to the deserts!" He said, "Baklava, basbousa, kunafeh… Oh, man, I can't wait!"

"Wow," Jamil said as he shook his head, "All this talk about food is making me hungry again, and we just had lunch! I thought Ramadan was about fasting!" He casually smacked Omar's arm, then tossed the ball again, "What about you?" He asked, "What do you guys do for Ramadan? Where is your family from again? Mexico?"

Omar rolled his eyes, "No. We're from Puerto Rico and Ecuador. And… well, I guess it is different for us. My parents converted, and I don't have any other Muslim family, so…"

His words trailed off as the bell sounded off loudly for class. "BEEEEEEEEP!" He did not even bother to finish his thought when everyone started rushing to their classrooms. The basketballs now rolled across the open court as eager children stumbled over them on their way to the open double doors.

3. CLOSE ENCOUNTER

OMAR WALKED down the hallway of An-Noor Academy slowly on purpose. Shiny red lockers lined the corridor, and the classroom doors were decorated with brightly colored paper and teachers' names in cutout letters.

Omar looked at the beige tiled floor and avoided every crack as he stepped. He almost lost his balance when he ran into something or someone. "Whoops!" He looked up to see Ms. Khan smiling with her white hijab studded with royal blue polka dots and enormous eyes, holding a stack of folders and papers. "I'm sorry, Ms. Kha... Khan...Excuse me. I was...I wasn't," Omar stammered.

"Looking where you were going?" Ms. Khan finished his sentence, "It's ok, sweetie. What's wrong? You seem a little distracted today. Are you ok?"

"Um... yes. I...I'm...yeah," Omar looked away, fidgeting with his hands, avoiding eye contact.

"Hm... I see," Ms. Khan exclaimed, "You know, after a semester and a half, I kind of know my students *pretty* well, Mr. Omar. And it seems to me that you do not like the assignment I gave you all today. Could that be the reason why you seem upset?"

Omar glanced up and back down. Ms. Khan was right. What could he say? He took a deep breath and spoke, "Well, it's not that I don't like the assignment. It's just that... I don't know what to write. My family is diff..."

"Say no more! It's ok, Omar. There is no right or wrong answer for this assignment. I tell you what, I'm going to give you a special tool that will make things easier for you,"

She searched through her papers and folders and pulled out a single sheet. "This is a bubble map. You may have seen these before," Ms. Khan explained. Omar looked up, "Like in first grade!" He thought aloud.

"Yes, but you know what? Even I still use these to gather my thoughts. I think they are one of the easiest and best brainstorming tools," Ms. Khan continued, "It is perfect for pre-writing. I want you to write Ramadan in the middle bubble, and then in the surrounding bubbles, write all the things that come to your mind. Add more bubbles if you need to and tie them all together.

Once you get an idea of all the wonderful things your family does during Ramadan, then just write it into your essay. Remember to write about your own experience. Do not focus on what everyone else is doing. This is all about you and your family."

Ms. Khan placed her hand on Omar's shoulder and bent down slightly, "I am really looking forward to hearing your presentation. You will do great! Now, go to your next class quickly."

Omar took the paper and forced a smile. As he shuffled away, Ms. Khan stood clutching her papers. She watched him thoughtfully as he disappeared into a nearby classroom.

4. BILINGUAL BRAINSTORM

LATER IN THE AFTERNOON, Omar arrived at his house after his dad picked him up from school in his polished burgundy pickup truck. *Papi* greeted him with his usual, "Salaamu alaikum, *mijo*!" but Omar stayed quiet the whole ride home.

When they pulled up into their driveway, Omar looked at his *casita*, his little house. It was a charming rancher with lemon meringue-colored stucco walls and orange terracotta shingles. He could see his little sister, María, playing in the backyard through the chain-link fence.

There was something magical about his home. Once he entered its warm walls, everything became bilingual – English and Spanish. He went inside and set his book bag down in the *sala*, the living room.

Papi stayed *afuera* to take some tools out of his truck. He owned his own landscaping business, and he would often tell Omar about how he started off mowing lawns when he was Omar's age. His father's parents were immigrants from Ecuador, and his grandfather worked in landscaping, too.

After high school, Omar's dad studied business, and since he loved landscaping so much, he decided to start his own company. Now, he helps other immigrant families by offering them work. He learned about Islam through one of his business partners and converted right before Omar was born.

Mami, Omar's mom, was in the *cocina*, the kitchen, as usual. Unlike Papi, she was born in Puerto Rico and moved to the United States as a little girl. She spoke *inglés y español* fluently since she was a child. After she and Papi were married, he taught her about Islam, and she decided to convert, too. When she was not working at the hospital as a Spanish interpreter, Mami would be in the kitchen preparing her favorite dishes.

"*Salaamu alaikum, hola Mami*," Omar called out. "*Hola mi amor, wa alaikum salaam! Ven a comer,* come eat! Wash your hands first," She responded. When he finally propped into a wooden dining room chair with his bubble chart and pencil, she greeted him again with a big, fat kiss on the cheek and a bowl of fruit salad. "What have you got there?" Mami asked curiously as she went back to cutting peppers for her Puerto Rican *arroz con pollo*.

"I have to write a paper and present tomorrow," Omar shrugged. Mami continued cutting peppers and said, "Ah, and what is it about?" "Ramadan," Omar responded, "We have to talk about how we celebrate Ramadan."

"*Ay, subhanAllah!* Ramadan is coming," Mami exclaimed, "I must get the house ready. This place is a mess!" She put a hand on her hip as she shook her head and looked around concerned, then went back to chopping peppers again.

Omar wrote the word "Ramadan" in the bubble in the middle of his page, then his pencil moved towards one of the clouds connected to the right side. He looked up at Mami curiously and then back to his page. He slowly wrote the words, "clean the house," then sat back, sinking into the chair.

María came skipping in from the patio through the sliding doors leading to the dining room, "*Hola*, Omar," she said, "What is that?" She leaned over to look at his paper.

"It's a list of things to do to get ready for Ramadan," he responded.

"Yay! Ramadan! Mami, can you make the *luna*-shaped *galletas* you always bake?" Aisha asked as she swung towards Mami excited, "*Por favor*, pleaaaseee? And can we make paper streamers and *rosas* for the living room, and can we get a *piñata* for Eid?"

Omar's face lit up, "You're the best, María!" She tilted her head and looked at him confused as he began filling in more bubbles around the word Ramadan. "Piñata, moon-shaped cookies, paper streamers…"

"You're weird, Omar. Anyway, Mami, can you also make empanadas? I want *carne molida* and *pollo*, or you can make ones with *queso*. Are we going to the *tarawih* prayers after we break our fast every night? Can I get a new *vestido* with a matching hijab for Eid? I can't wait!" María was now almost begging, jumping up and down with her hands clasped on her chest in the middle of the kitchen.

Mami smiled as she wiped a plate dry with a kitchen towel decorated with yellow sunflowers. "*Claro que sí,*" she said, "Of course! I will make the ground beef, chicken, and cheese empanadas. I will make my special Eid empanadas and color the dough with annatto to make them beautiful and orange. I am going to make a menu for us with all my favorite Caribbean recipes, so I don't have to worry too much about what to cook.

Maybe we can invite our non-Muslim *familia* over to break fast with us and go break our fast at the masjid some days *para variar*. A little variety is good, and Mami needs a break, too." She winked as she swayed towards the cabinet to put away the colorful plate.

Omar kept writing, 'write a menu with Puerto Rican recipes, break our fast at the masjid, invite non-Muslim family, Eid empanadas'... Everything started to come together.

5. BEING LATINO

WHEN PAPI FINISHED organizing his tools in the garage and washed up, Mami called everyone to dinner. *La mesa* was all set; María helped mom put plates, glasses, and forks down on orange placemats with paper napkins.

The bright yellow arroz con pollo sat on the middle of the table in a *caldero*, a huge metal pot sprinkled with a confetti of green chopped cilantro and bits of roasted red bell pepper. In a nearby white ceramic bowl was a side of pinto beans that had been simmered to perfection. The aroma of seasoned chicken and spices filled the air. Omar inhaled and felt himself float onto his chair.

"Mmm… *Que rico*! Delicious!" He exclaimed. Mami grinned in delight, "*Gracias, mi amor*. Let me serve you a plate."

It was a family tradition to eat dinner together and discuss the events of the day. Papi took turns asking everyone what was on their minds, how they spent their time, and what plans they had for tomorrow.

María, who was in first grade, yapped about what girl she was no longer friends with and why. For some strange reason, there was always some gossip happening in first grade. "She's best friends with Laila now," María went on, "But I don't care because she is so annoying."

Mami quickly interrupted, "Don't say that, baby, that's not nice, and we don't want to backbite anyone. I'm sure Ayah can be friends with both you and Laila. You can be BFFs, *mejor amigas por siempre!*"

Omar drowned out the conversation. He stabbed a piece of chicken with his fork and swayed it back and forth like a pendulum. He was still thinking about his assignment and whether or not his teacher and classmates would understand his Latino family.

It was hard being different. He didn't feel Latino enough outside of his Islamic school, yet he did not feel Muslim enough in school because of his background.

Everyone else came from many generations of Muslim ancestors, yet he was the child of converts whose relatives were not Muslim. Maybe that was the reason they were never invited to Ramadan or Eid gatherings.

"*Mijo, mijo*… son," Papi called multiple times. Omar was so deep in thought that he had not heard him. "OMAR!"

Omar looked up, startled, "*Sí*, Papi," responding like an attentive soldier to his superior. His father chuckled. "That was some serious daydreaming you were doing there," he said, shaking his head. "What's on your mind?"

"I was just thinking about what I have to write for my homework," explained Omar, "I have to talk about how we celebrate Ramadan and then present it to the class."

"Sounds pretty simple," Papi said as he stuffed a spoonful of rice in his mouth. María snorted, "He doesn't think so," she teased, "He is sooo worried like he's gonna fail or something."

"No," Omar protested.

"Yes, he is, Papi, he was working on it earlier, and he didn't know what to write!" María was really pushing Omar's nerves now. He felt his face burning. He did not want to have this discussion with Papi.

Mami gestured to María, "María, ¡ya! Enough! It's Omar's turn to talk."

"What are you worried about?" Papi asked. He put his fork down and leaned forward as he did when he wanted to give his undivided attention, like when he watched a soccer game and his favorite team was playing.

Omar shifted in his chair nervously. He was not sure if he could put his feelings into words. Now, as he felt everyone's eyes on him, he had no choice but to come to terms with his emotions. He opened his mouth to begin and was surprised at how quickly his thoughts poured out,

"My teacher, Ms. Khan, she...she started asking the class about how their family celebrates Ramadan and I was scared she would ask me because we are not like everyone else. We are not Pakistani, or Arab or African," Omar explained, "But then she made it homework, and tomorrow we all have to present it in class.

I asked my friends about what their families do, and they do typical stuff from their culture. I'm the only Latino in class, and they can't even tell the difference between Mexico and all of South America!"

Papi started to laugh but stopped when Mami kicked his leg under the table. Omar continued, "I didn't know what I was going to write, but I think I know now. Mami and María were talking about their plans for Ramadan, and I took some notes. So, it's fine, I guess."

Papi leaned back and took a deep breath, then nodded as he exhaled. "I get it *mijo*," he said, "I understand what you are feeling, but there is nothing to be worried about; *no te preocupes*. Don't you

37

know there are millions of Muslims in South America? Ramadan is just as much ours as everyone else's. Just because there aren't any other Latino kids in your school doesn't mean we don't exist. It's ok to be different; in fact, it's even better."

Mami nodded and added, "Look at me, I'm one of only two Spanish interpreters in the hospital during the day, and we help so many people. All the staff is always grateful to have us around because we are important. The same goes for the Islamic community. It is made up of people from all over the world, and we all bring value to the community."

Omar had not thought of it that way. "That's true," he said, "But most of our family isn't Muslim, and so we don't really celebrate things like my friends do. They have huge extended families that come together for Ramadan, or they send gifts from their countries. We don't have that."

"Sure, we do," Papi explained, "We also have relatives back home, and they visit us and send gifts, maybe not for Ramadan, but that's ok. Our family is creating our own traditions for Ramadan. And that makes it unique. We get to make our Ramadan extra special, and our family that's not Muslim gets to see that and experience it. They learn from us. I bet your friends and their families would love that opportunity."

6. THE WAIT

AFTER *LA CENA*, or dinner, Omar went to his room to work on his essay. He felt much more at ease after talking to his family. He sat on the lime green swivel chair Papi bought him for his *escritorio*. As he sat at his desk, he wrote at the top of his paper, "How My Family Celebrates Ramadan." He looked at his bubble chart and began extracting ideas to add to his essay one by one.

Before he knew it, he filled three pages! He read it and reread it to make sure he had not made any mistakes. When he was satisfied, he smiled to himself and felt a sense of relief. "Wow," he exclaimed out loud, "Finally!"

Even though he did not think his family's way of celebrating was anywhere close to Jamil's and Sami's, he was still proud that his family had their own traditions.

Omar was glad that Ms. Khan had given him the bubble graph after all. He put his papers inside a folder in his bookbag and got ready for bed.

The following day, as Omar walked into the school building once again, he felt his nerves gnawing away at the pit of his stomach like hungry caterpillars who would eventually turn to butterflies. He knew he would have to get up in front of the class during the third period and read his essay. Although he was confident about what he wrote, he was still unsure how it would be received.

Omar breezed through his math class, busying himself with worksheets on fractions and decimals. He wished life were always as easy as math; once you have the right formula, every problem was a breeze. His next period was history.

Coincidentally, the teacher began a new unit on the indigenous people of the Americas. His mind wandered, imagining himself living among the Incas in the Andes mountains, building forts made of limestone and granite with a llama by his side.

Just as he was thinking about what he would name her, the bell for third period rang.

As Omar made his way to Ms. Khan's English class, the caterpillars in his stomach, who had settled into their chrysalises during math and history, emerged again as butterflies. "Ugh," he thought. He breathed in slowly and sunk into his desk, "Here goes."

7. CLASSROOM DREAD

MS. KHAN'S KOHL EYES scanned the room as she sat waiting for the bell to signal the start of the third period. She made eye contact with Omar and smiled. He smiled back shyly and felt the flurry of butterflies again. Once everyone was settled, she shot up.

"Today is a special day!" She sang as she glided to the front of the room. Ms. Khan's demeanor was just as bubbly as the color of her hijabs. On this day, she chose a scarf with red and orange tones that reminded Omar of ripe mangos from Puerto Rico.

"When I call your name, please come up so you can share with us how your family celebrates Ramadan," She said.

One by one, Omar's classmates walked to the front of the class to read their essays as Ms. Khan called them by their last names in alphabetical order.

He listened to stories of shiny Moroccan lanterns, Turkish pre-dawn breakfast meals, Arabian dates soaked in water, Qur'an reading competitions, Indian rose-flavored pink milk for breaking the fast, Senegalese aunties cooking together, and huge Egyptian dinner parties. Omar was tense in his chair. Everyone's stories sounded so wonderfully foreign. How could he top any of them?

Every time Ms. Khan called another name, the butterflies in Omar's stomach fluttered more violently, making him nauseous. Surprisingly, however, when she got to the letter H, she skipped over Omar.

"How can this be?" He thought. He frowned and looked at Ms. Khan. If she would call him, at least he could get it over with.

She nodded and said, "Omar, I want you to go last if you don't mind."

"Great," he thought, letting out a sigh. The torture would continue. "But why?" Omar wondered. Maybe the lunch bell would ring, and class will be dismissed before his turn. "Oh, no, but today is

Friday," Omar thought fretfully, "We stay here for lunch!"

Due to the congregational prayer, on Fridays, Omar's class stayed in Ms. Khan's classroom for lunch and recess before going to prayer. That meant that she could make the class last as long as she wanted! He was in trouble.

Sweat started dripping from Omar's forehead. More of his classmates stood up to talk about their Ramadan, but he could no longer hear what they were saying. He was too consumed in his own thoughts.

Finally, once everyone had their turn, all eyes turned curiously towards Omar. He was resting his head on his closed fist like The Thinker statue he learned about in art class. He wished he were a statue at that moment.

"Omar," called Ms. Khan, "Mr. Omar, your turn, my dear!" Omar took a deep breath and thought about Papi's words, *"It's ok to be different; in fact, it's even better!"*

He willed himself out of his chair, ignoring the butterflies who had now made a permanent home of his gut and walked to the front of the room with his papers in hand. He faced all his classmates. They were attentive, eager to hear his story, especially since Ms. Khan wanted him to go last. They also wondered why.

Omar took another deep breath before he began speaking.

8. RAMADAN LATINO STYLE

"HOW MY FAMILY CELEBRATES RAMADAN"
By Omar Hernandez

My family is not what people would say is a typical Muslim family. When people think about Muslims, they usually picture Arabs or South Asians. But my father taught me that Allah created everyone to worship Him, no matter where they are from. Islam is all over the world. This includes Latin America, where my parents were born. When we celebrate, it may look different, but Ramadan is the same for all of us.

Just like all other Muslims, we prepare for Ramadan by making our intention to fast. We make plans to read the Quran daily and pray tarawih. My mother thinks it's important to welcome Ramadan with a clean heart and a clean house, so she makes sure that our home looks and smells nice.

Then, we decorate the house with paper streamers and roses made from tissue paper. Sometimes we make lanterns out of colorful construction paper to hang up on the ceiling like our Middle Eastern friends do. We also cut out the phrase, "Feliz Ramadán," or Happy Ramadan, out of decorative cardboard and thread the letters together to form a banner. We drape it across the window with string lights.

One of my favorite things my parents do is hang a piñata in the middle of the living room. Piñatas are popular in our culture. They can be made in many shapes, and we fill them with candy and small toys. You can either make your own with cardboard covered in bits of tissue paper or buy one from a store. After Ramadan, on Eid, we take turns trying to break the piñata with a stick so the candy spills out. My dad puts a blindfold on me and spins me around, so I get dizzy before my turn. We all laugh, and my mom takes pictures.

Another way we celebrate Ramadan is by planning what foods we will eat to break our fast

each day. My mom likes to cook all our favorite
Puerto Rican dishes like arroz con habichuelas *(rice*
and beans), arroz con pollo *(rice with chicken),*
rellenos de papa *(stuffed potato balls),* pasteles
(turnovers made from plantains and green bananas),
and tostones *(fried plantains). We break our fast*
daily with our traditional food, although some days
we go to the mosque and eat there. Other days, we
have non-Muslim family over for dinner, like my
abuela, *grandmother, or uncles. They bring us food*
and wait for us to break our fast so we can eat
together.

During the month, we try our best to pray
tarawih prayers at the mosque every day. At home,
we sit together on the floor an hour before breaking
our fast so we can read from the Qur'an. We take
turns reading parts in Arabic, English, and Spanish.

For Eid, my mom bakes cakes with guava
filling and moon-shaped sugar cookies decorated
with frosting and sprinkles. We share those with
family, friends, and neighbors. But out of all the food
we have during this time, my most favorite of all are

empanadas, *fried turnovers stuffed with meat or cheese. To me, they look like crescent moons and are the best treat for iftar and especially for Eid. Even our non-Muslim family members love to come over for some Eid empanadas! This is how we celebrate.* Felíz Ramadán... *that means Happy Ramadan.*

9. THE EMPANADAS

"**FELÍZ RAMADÁN!**" Sami shouted! Other classmates joined him, "Felíz Ramadán, Omar!" "That is so cool. I want to learn Spanish," Mustafa said. "Me too," said Haifa, "Can you teach us, Omar?" "Yeaaaa!!!" chimed in some of the other students.

"Ok, settle down now," Ms. Khan said, waving a hand back and forth, "JazakAllah khaiyr, Omar, may Allah reward you for such a great presentation. And same to everyone."

Omar felt so relieved. Even the butterflies were gone. He smiled to himself as he made his way back to his seat, and Ms. Khan took his place in the front of the room.

Jamil leaned over to him, "Seriously, you do have to teach me some Spanish!" "I got you," agreed Omar.

Ms. Khan was still addressing the class, "Now, since Ramadan is starting in a couple of days and today is Friday, the last school day before we start fasting, I have a treat for you." "Woohooo!" cried out Ayesha, then quickly covered her mouth and said, "Sorry!"

Ms. Khan rolled her eyes, smiling, and continued, "Like I was saying, I have a special treat. Last night I called Ms. Hernandez, Omar's mother, and I asked her if she would bring some of her Eid empanadas so we could taste them."

Omar's eyes widened as he glanced over to the door just as his mother was stepping into the classroom carrying a huge tray wrapped in aluminum foil.

He felt his cheeks turn red and looked away. "Ma!" He protested under his breath. Mami looked at him apologetically and shrugged. She knew he would be embarrassed but could not say no when Ms. Khan called her the previous night and requested that she bring Omar's favorite Ramadan-inspired dish to share with the class.

Luckily, it was her day off, and she was able to make the empanadas after Omar and María went to school.

Mami set the tray down on a table in the back of the classroom and went out to fetch another. Ms. Khan helped her set down a second tray, and they removed the foil from the tops.

Suddenly, the smell of delicious spices and fried dough filled the air. About 100 empanadas sat in neat golden and orange lines. The kids were oohing and aahing, then Ms. Khan cleared her throat and said, "Ahem, class? How do we greet a guest?"

"As salaamu alaikum, Ms. Hernandez!" They shouted harmoniously. Mami smiled and responded, "Wa alaikum salaam. Nice to meet you all." She glanced at Omar, who was still looking away. As she placed some paper plates and napkins on the table, Ms. Khan asked inquisitively, "Could you tell us what you brought for us?"

Mami said, "Well, these are my special Eid empanadas. They are Puerto Rican hand pies or dumplings that are stuffed with a variety of fillings. I brought 3 different types: ground beef, shredded chicken, and cheese. These are fried, although there are also baked varieties from all over Latin America."

"They sound delicious! JazakiAllah khaiyr, may Allah reward you for coming. Let us give them a try!" Ms. Khan exclaimed. Omar's classmates were excited and squealing in delight.

They could not wait to taste the yummy-looking crescent-shaped treats. Ms. Khan instructed them to go row by row, two students at a time to grab 1, 2, and 3 empanadas, one of each flavor.

When it was Omar's turn, he also stood up and grabbed a plate. As he passed by his mother, he gave her a quick side hug and said, "Salaamu alaikum, Mami. *Gracias*." Mami beamed.

10. NEW TRADITIONS

THE ROOM FELL SILENT after everyone had gotten their empanadas. The students sniffed and stared at them before taking careful nibbles and then full-blown bites. Omar became nervous again.

He hoped that his classmates appreciated his favorite food. After all, he ate the Mediterranean and South Asian foods often served at gatherings in the masjid. Couldn't they also enjoy Latino food? Omar's thoughts were interrupted when his classmates began blurting out their reactions.

"Oh my… this is sooo good," Maryam said.

Ms. Khan agreed, "They are really good! Mmm. So flavorful!"

"It's like a samosa," declared Ali, pointing his finger up as if he just solved a mystery. Ayman nodded.

"It's better than a samosa," exclaimed Sami with his mouth full, "It's not spicy, so I can actually eat it! All my problems have been solved!" Everyone snorted in amusement.

"Bro, I can't stop eating," Jamil added, "Anyone who doesn't want theirs, I am accepting donations!" At this point, even Omar was laughing.

"Ok, that's it! I need the recipe, Ms. Hernandez, so I can give it to my mom," said Ayesha.

"Yes, me too, but for myself," laughed Ms. Khan.

Mami was ecstatic. She, like Omar, was so relieved that everyone liked their style of cooking. Omar could not stop smiling. It was heartwarming to see his teacher and all his classmates enjoying his favorite holiday dish.

Wanting to share the experience with them, he bit into a warm beef empanada and felt its delicious juices trickle down the side of his lip. They really were tasty. Suddenly, Omar felt a pair of hands rest on his shoulders.

He looked up and saw Ms. Khan's joyful face looking down at him. She knelt beside him, handed him a napkin, and whispered, "See? I told you that you would do great!" She ruffled his hair as she stood up and asked the class, "Who needs another napkin?"

Mami had made so many empanadas that Ms. Khan was able to share them with other teachers and school staff. By the end of the day, everyone at An-Noor Islamic Academy was raving about the Eid empanadas.

That Ramadan, the Hernandez family received numerous invitations to break the fast with other Muslim families from the community. Mothers and aunties asked Mami for recipes, while their husbands talked to Papi about Islam and Latin America over *cafecito* or chai.

Omar's classmates and friends all begged him to teach them Spanish words while María taught their younger siblings how to play dominoes. For Eid, Mami and Papi planned to prepare empanadas to take to the mosque.

Omar and his family continued to build new holiday traditions, and best of all, they would never have to spend Ramadan and Eid alone again.

Bonus: Latino Eid Poem

THE MONTH OF RAMADAN is almost here,

Our favorite time of the year.

Men and women, boys and girls,

Little Muslims all around the world.

That think nothing can be better,

Than fasting and praying together.

Children with names like Abdullah and Ibrahim,

Laila, Ayesha, Musa, Mustafa, and Shireen.

But there is something I have to say,

It is a little different for a kid named Jose.

While other families go to the masjid,

He and his family say *mezquita* instead.

When you break your fast with samosas,

They munch on *empanadas muy, muy sabrosas*.

And when it is time to spread greetings,

They will wish everyone a Ramadan and Eid feliz!

You see, Muslims are not all the same,

They come from countries with all kinds of names.

Some are from Australia, Africa, Europe, and Asia,

Countries like the UK, Sweden, Syria, and Malaysia,

And in case you and your friends did not know,

There are lots from Latin America, also.

While some Muslims speak Arabic fluently,

Others speak Italian, Turkish, and Hindi,

Portuguese, English, Urdu, and Mandarin,

And like Jose and his family, some speak *español,*

también.

Many countries, colors, and languages are great,

When what brings us all together is our faith.

We can all pray and learn, you and me,

Because you cannot have community without

UNITY!

Glossary of Spanish words and phrases

Abuela – grandmother

Afuera – outside

Amigas por siempre – best friends forever

Arroz con habichuelas – rice with beans

Arroz con pollo – rice with chicken

Cafecito – a small cup of coffee, a diminutive form of the work *café*, which means coffee

Caldero – cooking pot, cauldron

Carne molida – ground meat (typically refers to beef)

Casita – small house, diminutive form of the word *casa* or house

Claro que sí – Of course!

Cocina – kitchen

Empanada – A Latin-American turnover, hand pie, or dumpling; a stuffed pastry which is fried or baked

Escritorio – desk

Español – Spanish

Familia – family

Feliz Ramadán – happy Ramadan

Galletas – cookies

Gracias – thank you

Hola – hello, hi

Inglés – English

La cena – dinner

La mesa – the table

Luna – moon

Mami – Mommy, mom, a diminutive form of the word *madre* or mother

Mezquita – mosque, a place where Muslims worship.

Mi amor – my love

Mijo – son, short for "My son" or *Mi hijo*

Muy – very

Muy sabrosas – very tasty

No te preocupes – Don't worry

Papi – Daddy, Dad, a diminutive form of the word *padre* or father

Para variar – for a change, to vary

Pasteles – in Puerto Rico these are turnovers made of green bananas, plantains, and taro root stuffed with ground meat, wrapped in palm leaves, and steamed or boiled

Piñata – a decorative container usually made of cardboard or papier-mâché covered in tissue paper that is filled with candy or trinkets and is suspended and broken as part of a celebration

Pollo – chicken

Por favor – please

Que rico – delicious

Queso – cheese

Rellenos de papa – stuffed potatoes

Rosas – roses

Sala – living room, sitting room

Sí – yes

También – Also, too

Tostones – fried plantain discs

Ven – come

Ven a comer – come to eat, come eat

Vestido – dress

Y - and

Ya – Enough

Glossary of Islamic terms

An-Noor – Arabic for "the light."

Eid – a Muslim holiday or festival, one of two Muslim holidays: Eid-al-fitr and Eid-al-Adha (the festival marking the end of the annual pilgrimage to Mecca or Hajj)

Eid-al-fitr – the festival of the breaking of the fast, an Islamic holiday that takes place on the first day of Shawwal, the 10th month of the Islamic lunar calendar, marking the end of the Ramadan fasting month.

Hijab – a covering, the veil of the Muslim woman, often used synonymously with headscarf or veil

Insha'Allah – Arabic for "God willing," an expression often used in place of "hopefully."

JazakAllah khaiyr – May God reward you with good (Other forms include *jazakiAllah khaiyr* to a woman or *jazakumAllahu khaiyran* – may Allah reward all of you with good)

Masjid – mosque; a place where Muslims worship.

Ramadan – the 9th month in the Islamic lunar calendar in which Muslims engage in fasting from dawn to sunset and extra forms of worship like prayer, giving in charity, and reading the Quran (Koran).

Salaamu alaikum – the Islamic greeting meaning "May peace be upon you."

SubhanAllah – Glory be to God, often used to express surprise or praise

Tarawih – the nightly congregational prayer performed in the month of Ramadan, during which the Quran is divided into sections to recite it in its entirety during the month.

Wa alaikum salaam – the response to the Islamic greeting *As salaamu alaikum* or *Salaamu alaikum*, and it means "May peace be upon you, also"

From My Cocina to Yours

After reading all about Eid empanadas, I am sure you would like to try them. Well, here is a special treat for you and your family – my very own empanada recipe!

Before I share the recipe, let me tell you a little bit about why I love empanadas. When I began learning about Islam, I met people from many different countries. I was exposed to a wide range of cultures. I soon realized that something we all have in common is FOOD. Although our foods may look similar, they have different flavors and methods of preparation.

One of these ethnically diverse dishes is dumplings – hand pies or pastries stuffed with spiced meats and or vegetables, cheese, or even nuts and fruit. The Puerto Rican variety is called an *empanada* or *empanadilla*. When South Asians ask me what they are, I tell them they are like a Spanish version of a samosa! One thing is for sure; these delectable treats are a hit no matter where in the world we are from.

In Puerto Rico, street vendors sell empanadas just about everywhere, including corner stores, beachside, and even outside homes. The dough can be golden brown or orange from the annatto used for coloring. I learned how to make empanadas from my *Mami*.

We do not tend to write down the specific amount of each ingredient we use in our cooking. Instead, we prepare our empanadas with lots of love by tossing in each component and seasoning to our desired taste. This freedom gives the empanadas varying flavors depending on who is cooking.

73

Empanadas have become a staple for Ramadan iftars and other community events in my family as we preserve our Latino culture while practicing Islam. We hope now they can also become a tradition in your kitchen.

Puerto Rican Empanadas or Empanadillas

Ingredients:

2 packages of premade discs for empanadas, 20 count
(You can also make your own with 3 cups of flour, 1/3
cup vegetable or corn oil, 1 1/2tsp salt, 1tsp sugar, 1 cup
of warm water – mix to form a dough adding flour as
needed to prevent stickiness, knead, divide and flatten
with a rolling pin and press out discs with the edge of a
bowl or cup)

1 green pepper chopped

1 red pepper chopped

1 small onion chopped

2 garlic cloves chopped

Cilantro

Oregano (optional)

Pimento stuffed green olives chopped (optional)

Adobo Powder

1 package of Sazon or 1 tsp Turmeric for color (optional)

1 large tomato chopped or can be substituted by half a
small can of plain tomato sauce, or 2 Tbsp tomato paste

1 lb. Ground or finely chopped halal meat or seafood
(beef, chicken, shrimp etc.)

1 medium boiled potato in cubes (optional)

Vegetable or corn oil (for frying)

Directions:

1. Sautee onion, green and red pepper for a minute or two, add garlic and meat, adobo, sazon/turmeric on high heat or medium/high. Brown the meat, then add tomato or tomato sauce/paste. Once the meat is cooked, lower heat to medium.

2. Add chopped cilantro, olives, and oregano to taste. Cook for another 2 minutes and turn off the heat. Add potato cubes (potato helps to absorb excess moisture and oil). Let sit until you are ready to stuff. You may refrigerate the meat until you are ready for the next step.

3. Begin preparing your empanadas for frying. Add 2 Tbsp or so of the meat mixture to the center of a flour disc.

4. Fold into a half-moon shape, seal the edges by pressing down with a fork, flip over and seal again.

5. After sealing front and back, set aside until cooking oil in the frying pan is hot. The empanadas are ready for frying when the oil bubbles when putting the handle of a wooden spoon inside.

6. Fry 3 or 4 (depending on the size of your pan) at once. Once you see one side is golden brown, flip over carefully.

7. When both sides have cooked evenly, remove from the pan and place on a rack or paper towel to drain excess oil.

Serve with "Mayoketchup" (Mayonaisse, ketchup, finely chopped garlic or garlic powder mixture)

Note: For cheese empanadas, use shredded mozzarella cheese and follow steps 3-7.

Enjoy!

This recipe yields approximately 20 empanadas.

About the Author

WENDY DÍAZ was born in Puerto Rico, where she spent half of her childhood before moving to the United States. She is an award-winning poet, author, translator, and co-founder of Hablamos Islam – a social project focused on creating educational resources about Islam in the Spanish language. After graduating from the University of Maryland, Baltimore County, with a degree in modern languages and linguistics, she began her career as a teacher. However, when she discovered her passion for creative writing and storytelling, she decided to devote her efforts to creating unique children's stories. Wendy has published over ten children's books and currently resides in Maryland with her family.

Read more about Wendy Díaz at hablamosislam.org and follow her on Facebook and Instagram @authorwendydiaz and @HablamosIslam.

For more books by Wendy Díaz, visit amazon.com/author/wendydiaz